STOOEY THE POOEY TUI

WRITTEN AND ILLUSTRATED BY PAUL ELDER

Stooey the Pooey Tui

Written and Illustrated
by
Paul Elder

I was walking in the forest one day
and I saw a bird, who liked to poop...

Ker-splat!

and was quite crazy.

He was Stooey the Screwy, Pooey Tui.

I was walking in a forest one day
and I saw a bird, who liked to poop...

Ker-splat!

was quite crazy
and was a snappy dresser

He was Stooey the Groovy,
Screwy, Pooey Tui

I was walking in the forest
one day and I saw a bird,
who liked to poop...

Ker-splat!

was quite crazy,
was a snappy dresser and
liked to perform
dive bombs.

He was Stooey the Swoopy,
Groovy, Screwy,
Pooey Tui

I was walking through the forest one day and I saw a bird, who liked to poop...

Ker-splat!

was quite crazy. was a snappy dresser, liked to perform dive bombs and spoke lots of gibberish.

He was Stooey the Hooey,
Swoopy, Groovy, Screwy, Pooey Tui.

I was walking in the forest one day
and I saw a bird, who liked to poop...

Ker-splat!

was quite crazy, was a snappy dresser,
liked to perform dive bombs,
spoke lots of gibberish
and was really nosey.

He was Stooey the Snoopy, Hooey, Swoopy, Groovy, Screwy, Pooey Tui.

I was walking in the forest one day
and I saw a bird, who liked to poop...

Ker-splat!

was quite crazy, was a snappy dresser,
liked to perform dive bombs,
spoke lots of gibberish,
was really nosey
and sometimes liked to jeer

He was Stooey the Booey, Snoopy, Hooey, Swoopy, Groovy, Screwy, Pooey Tui.

I was walking in the forest one day
and I saw a bird, who liked to poop...

Ker-splat!

was quite crazy, was a snappy dresser,
liked to perform dive bombs,
spoke lots of gibberish,
was really nosey,
sometimes liked to jeer
and whose poop was really sticky!

He was Stooey the Gooey, Booey, Snoopy, Hooey, Swoopy, Groovy, Screwy, Pooey Tui

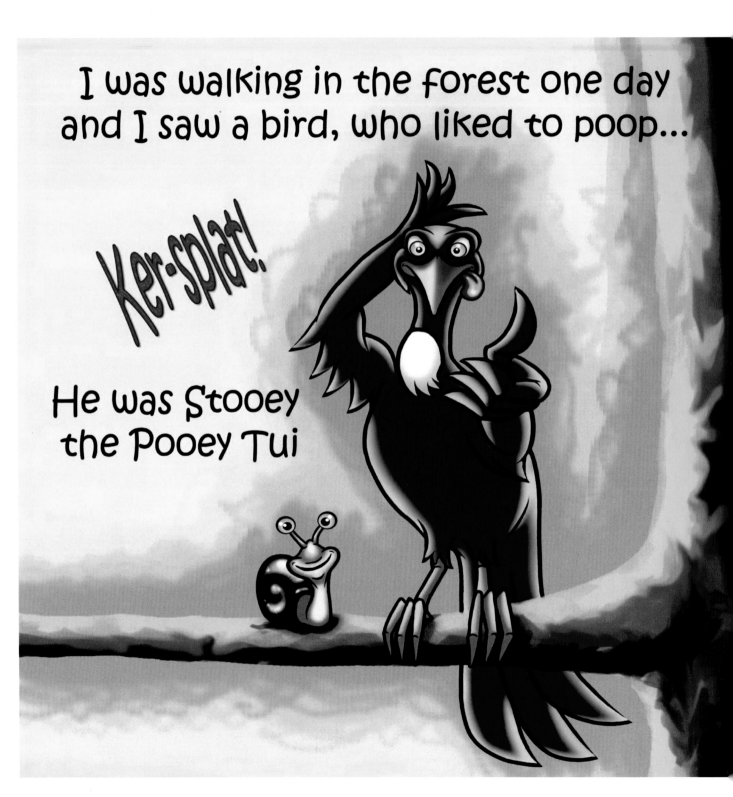

The End

www.hairytrolldesignz.com

Illustrations by Hairytroll Designz
Contact: paulelder@hairytrolldesignz.com

Thank you so much for taking the time to read
this book, I hope you enjoyed it, so much so
that you feel a review would be in order.

Reviews help make better books for the future.

Coming Soon!

Written & Illustrated
by
Paul Elder

If you enjoyed 'Stooey the Pooey Tui'
Then why not take a look at these
other books?

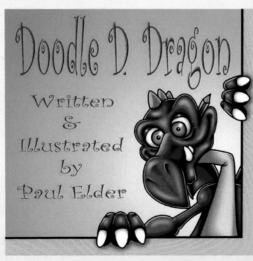

How to draw Stooey!

So you liked the book?

Want to know how to draw
Stooey the Pooey Tui?

Okay!

You will need some Paper
A Pencil
an Eraser
(just in case we make some mistakes)

Let's start with the base...

This is the very basic shapes
that go together to make up
Stooey.

We have a circle for his head
His neck is two straight lines
attached to another circle
(this circle has been squished a bit
to make Stooey's body a little bit longer)

Then some lines that will make his legs

Stooey's head:

So we have drawn over the circle that we
started with, to add eyes,
a beak, eyebrows and a cheeky smile

Stooey's wings:

The wing closest to the front
we have made flat to his body

But his other wing we have made into
a 'thumbs up' shape, Stooey can fold
his feathers to make fingers

Real Birds can't do this.....
so don't ask them to give you the 'thumbs up' sign
They might just look at you strange

Stooey's legs:

All we have done is add some extra lines
to make up the toes and Stooey's skinny legs

He has three toes to the front and a single
toe to the back that enables him to keep
hold of the branch..

Stooey's tail:

What would Stooey be without his long tail feathers?

Well Stooey, without his long tail feathers....

Just a few liness to add a luxurious tail

12961424R00020